Best wishes,

Alexander McCall Smith.

'When the lion noticed the tin dog, it stood quite still. Unconcerned, the tin dog gave a friendly bark and trotted over the sawdust floor, his tail wagging in friendliness.

"Get that dog out of there!" the ringmaster cried. "Quick, before it's too late!"

Uncle George rose to his feet and called out to the tin dog. But it was already too late. Before the tin dog could realize what was happening, the giant tin lion had opened its great jaws, pounced, and swallowed him up completely. Then the lion sat back, licked its lips and roared loudly.'

Tim is overjoyed when his Uncle George makes him a very special present – a tin dog. He has always wanted a dog of his own! Together they have a lot of fun. But then Tim and Uncle George take the tin dog along to the circus . . .

THE
Tin Dog

ALEXANDER McCALL SMITH

Illustrated by Jon Riley

YOUNG CORGI BOOKS

THE TIN DOG

A YOUNG CORGI BOOK 0 552 52607X

First published in Great Britain by Young Corgi Books

PRINTING HISTORY
Young Corgi edition published 1990
Reprinted 1991

This book is set in 14/18pt Century Schoolbook by
Kestrel Data, Exeter

Young Corgi Books are published by Transworld Publishers
Ltd., 61–63 Uxbridge Road, Ealing, London W5 5SA, in
Australia by Transworld Publishers (Australia) Pty. Ltd., 15–23
Helles Avenue, Moorebank, NSW 2170, and in New Zealand by
Transworld Publishers (N.Z.) Ltd., Cnr. Moselle and Waipareira
Avenues, Henderson, Auckland.

Made and printed in Great Britain by
The Guernsey Press Co. Ltd, Guernsey, Channel Islands.

This book is for André, Louisa,
and Cara

Chapter One

Tim lived with his aunt in a house
which was always kept just so. Other
houses usually have a bit of dust lying
about, or a mess where people have
forgotten to put things away, but
Tim's house was never like that. You
could walk into it at any time of the
day, or even in the middle of the night,
and find everything as tidy as you
could imagine.

'Never forget to scrub out the bath,'

Tim's aunt would say to him, wagging a thin finger in his face. 'Never leave the top of the toothpaste off. Never forget to put your shoes back in the cupboard (with the toes pointing towards the front). And never, ever come into the house with mud on your boots.'

Mud! Even the word made Tim's aunt shudder as she uttered it.

Tim, of course, had no choice but to be tidy. He wasn't very happy about it and, in fact, the whole house had a rather sad feel to it. It wasn't a place in which you could relax, a place where you could sneak your feet up on to the furniture and feel at home. It was a bit like staying in a hotel, Tim thought, or a palace perhaps. It was quite unlike other people's houses, where Tim had always noticed a lot of things lying about and even, in one or two very comfortable houses, a bit of mud here and there.

As well as having his aunt, Tim had an uncle who lived only three or four houses away. Uncle George, who was his tidy aunt's brother, lived in a very different sort of house. His garden was always full of weeds, with stray cats lurking behind the bushes, and sometimes the odd rat scurrying away behind the garage. Wherever you went inside there was the most marvellous mess and muddle. In the hallway there were old umbrellas and sticks with seats on them. In the corridor there were pegs hung with coats that looked as if they hadn't been worn for years. In the living-room there were bundles of papers and all sorts of interesting-looking boxes, some of them tied up with string, the others full of extraordinary bits and pieces. And in the kitchen . . . well, it's probably best not to say too much about that.

Uncle George looked as untidy as his house. His chin was always covered with prickly stubble which he had forgotten to shave off. His hair, which went in all directions, never seemed to be brushed or combed, and you could tell what he had had for lunch that day just by looking at the stains on his shirt. And yet, in the middle of all the stubble and the stains and the hair, there was a smile which made you completely forget about how messy he looked.

Tim loved to visit his Uncle George. Together they would fiddle about with one of the models which his uncle liked to make, spending hours sticking the parts together and

winding up the mechanisms of the clockwork machines which Uncle George sold to shops and collectors. Hours could pass that way, until there would be a knock on the door and Tim's aunt would appear telling him to come home.

'George!' she would shout at the front door. 'Send that boy back immediately! Don't you realize it's bad for him to spend so much time in all that filthy mess!'

Uncle George would smile.

'In a moment,' he would call back. 'In a moment.'

He knew that his sister would never come into the house and that if he kept her waiting at the door long enough she might see a rat. That would send her racing home, and he and Tim would have a few more hours fiddling about with all the bits and pieces.

One day Uncle George asked Tim why he didn't have a dog.

'I'd love one,' Tim replied sadly. 'I've asked Aunt Mag for one, but all she does is shudder and say that dogs are far too messy.'

Uncle George nodded his head. 'I can imagine that,' he said. 'Did she say it would leave hairs all over the house?'

'Yes,' said Tim. 'And she also said that it would bring in fleas and leave bones about the place.'

'There's nothing wrong with fleas,' mused Uncle George. And as for bones . . . have you ever noticed what a nice smell a good old bone has? It's a rich smell, a warm one. I'm not surprised that dogs like bones so much.'

He was silent for a moment. Then, quite suddenly, he stood up and scratched his head. Tim had seen Uncle George get ideas before and he knew that this was what was happening. When a very brilliant idea came to him – an idea for a particularly good gadget or something like that – he would close his eyes and scratch his head vigorously. This was exactly what was happening now, and Tim knew that his uncle liked to be left alone at such times.

Quietly saying goodbye, Tim left the house. He knew that if he came back a day or two later, he would see the result of Uncle George's idea. And whatever it was, it was bound to be a great deal of fun.

Chapter Two

It was three days before Tim was able to visit Uncle George again. He found it difficult to contain his excitement and when Uncle George opened the door he couldn't help blurting out a question.

'Have you made it?' he asked. 'Have you finished?'

Uncle George looked puzzled. 'Made what?' he asked. 'Finished what?'

'Whatever it is,' Tim said. 'The

thing you were thinking about.'

Uncle George smiled. 'Oh that!' he said. 'The . . . er . . . the whatnot. Yes, that's finished.' He paused and looked at Tim. 'Would you like to see it?'

'Of course I would,' said Tim.

'Well, you shall see it then,' said Uncle George. 'I made it for you, after all.'

Tim followed his uncle down the corridor and into the workroom where the models were made. It was more of a mess than usual, with bits of wire littering the floor and nuts and bolts on every surface. As he entered the room, Tim saw a large box on the workbench.

'That's it,' said Uncle George. 'Or rather, that's its box. The thing itself . . . the . . . er . . . the . . . well, it's inside.'

Tim crossed to the workbench and carefully began to lift the box down to the floor. It wasn't light, and he had to be careful because whatever was inside moved slightly as the box tilted.

'Be careful,' warned Uncle George. 'Open the top cautiously.'

Slowly Tim took the top off the box and peered inside. As he did so, he caught his breath. He had never before seen anything quite like this. It was perfect.

'Uncle George!' he whistled. 'However did you make it? It's . . . it's . . .'

'It's a tin dog,' said Uncle George, in a matter-of-fact voice. 'If you take it out – carefully – you can turn it on.'

Tim reached into the box and lifted out the dog. Then, placing it on the floor, he bent down to examine it more closely. It was the most beautiful

model he had ever seen, with tin sides that had been carefully painted to look like the coat of a real dog, and with legs that had joints in them in exactly the places where a real dog would bend its knees. There was a tail, which was hinged on to the body, a head with eyes made of glass, and a mouth that could be prised open to reveal a perfect set of tin teeth.

'If you look in the front,' Uncle George said, 'you'll find the switch. Yes, that's it.'

Gingerly Tim moved the small switch on the dog's chest and then stood back. For a moment or two nothing happened, and he glanced at Uncle George in a disappointed way.

'Warming up,' Uncle George said. 'Just you watch . . .'

Before Uncle George had time to

finish what he was saying, the tin dog suddenly started to move. It was a small movement at first, no more than a twitch of the tail and the slightest nodding of the head, but then, with a little growl, it put one leg in front of the other and began to walk towards Tim.

Tim stood quite still as the tin dog came up to him.

'He likes you,' Uncle George said. 'Look – he wants you to pat him.'

Tim bent down and patted the tin dog on its head. The dog seemed to like this for he gave a little bark of pleasure and his tin tail went from side to side, rather like the pendulum of a clock.

'He should be able to do everything real dogs can do,' Uncle George explained. 'In fact, I rather think he'll be able to do a bit more.'

'But how does he work?' Tim asked. He was used to his uncle making clever machines, but this one seemed to be quite remarkable.

Uncle George shrugged his shoulders. 'It's quite simple, really,' he said. 'But it would take an awfully long time to explain. All you have to remember is that he will need new batteries every two weeks and that you'll have to oil his legs and his tail.' Uncle George paused. 'And another thing,' he went on. 'Tin dogs go for ankles. Watch out for that. And also – and this is most important – don't let it get rusty.'

The tin dog had now sat down and was looking expectantly at Tim.

'He wants to go for a walk,' said Uncle George. 'I've bought you a lead for him – and a collar.'

Once the tin dog was safely attached to the lead, Tim took him out of the house and on to the street. Uncle George waved goodbye as they left the house and soon disappeared back into his workroom. His heart full of gratitude for his uncle's kind gift, Tim set off with the tin dog walking obediently at his side.

'At last,' he thought. 'At last I've got a dog of my own, even if it's only a tin one.'

The tin dog trotted along happily, his head nodding up and down as his tin legs moved backwards and forwards. And then, without any warning, he stopped.

The tin dog had seen a cat.

Chapter Three

The cat was perched on top of a wall, its fur raised in alarm, its eyes fixed on the tin dog below.

'Stay where you are!' Tim whispered to the cat. 'You're perfectly safe up there.'

As Tim spoke, the tin dog began to growl. At first he didn't make a very loud noise, but after a moment or two there was a whirring sound and his jaws opened. After this came a deep bark, the sort of bark normally made by dogs twice the size of the tin dog.

The sound of the bark disturbed the cat, which leapt in panic from the top of the wall and began to dash across the street. This was a mistake. Immediately the tin dog began to run after it, easily slipping the lead from Tim's hand.

Halfway across the street, the cat stopped to face its enemy. Its back arched, it stood its ground, hissing a warning, daring the tin dog to come one step closer.

'Come back!' shouted Tim. 'Come back here!'

The tin dog may have heard his master, but he decided to ignore him. As he took a further step forwards, the cat let out an awful yowl and swiped a paw at the tin dog's nose. All that

Tim heard was the sound of the cat's
claws scraping against the tin and
then a clicking sound.

The cat drew back its paw in
surprise. It had not expected to hit
something so smooth and so solid, and
its claws felt quite sore. But something had happened to the tin dog
himself, who now stood quite still, one
leg halfway off the ground, his jaw
stuck open.

For a moment Tim thought that the

dog was planning what to do, but then he realized that something quite different had happened. As the cat's paw hit the tin dog, it had brushed against the switch and had turned the dog off.

The cat looked puzzled. It hissed again and took another swipe at the immobile dog. Once again there was the sound of metal being hit and nothing else happened. The cat's eyes opened wide in surprise. This was a most peculiar dog, quite unlike any other dog it had seen before. It hissed again, but when there was no reaction it decided to slip away. This dog was obviously going to be no further trouble. Some dogs are taught their lesson very quickly, thought the cat.

After the cat had left, Tim turned the dog back on and continued on his way. The tin dog appeared to forget the cat immediately and behaved very well for the rest of the walk. Tim passed one or two people, but they ignored the tin dog. They were used to seeing dogs in the street and there was no reason for anybody to pay particular attention to this one. This suited Tim, who thought that the last thing he wanted was for his aunt to find out. It would be no use telling her that the tin dog didn't smell and wouldn't need to eat bones. In her mind, a dog was a dirty creature and the fact that the dog was made out of tin would make no difference at all.

Back home, Tim crept quietly upstairs, carrying the panting tin dog under his arm.

'Don't make a sound,' Tim whispered to the dog. The tin dog

looked up at his master and licked Tim's arm with his tin tongue.

Once he was safely in his room, Tim closed the door behind him and put the tin dog down. The dog wagged his tail and looked around the room. He seemed pleased with his new surroundings and immediately set about investigating them. He poked his nose into the wastepaper bin and sniffed. Then he stood up on his hind legs and looked up at the table. It was at this point that Tim heard footsteps on the stairs.

'Here!' he said, reaching out for the tin dog. 'It's my aunt!'

The dog must have thought that Tim wanted to play, for he immediately romped away from him and hid under the bed. Tim could just see the dog's tin nose sticking out from under the bed cover. He crossed the room towards it and was just about to reach under the bed to turn the dog's switch off when the door opened.

'What are you doing?' Tim's aunt asked. 'I thought I asked you to tidy this room up.'

'But it *is* tidy,' Tim protested, looking round at all his neatly laid-out possessions.

'Tidy!' exclaimed his aunt. 'Look over there. Look at that ruler lying on the table. How many times do I have to tell you . . .'

She stopped halfway through. From under the bed there had come an unmistakable growl. Tim's heart stopped.

'What was that?' asked his aunt, peering around suspiciously. 'I'm sure I heard something.'

Tim thought quickly. 'Oh, it's my tummy,' he said. 'I haven't had anything to eat for a long time and my tummy's started to rumble.'

'Well, tidy up first,' his aunt scolded.

She turned to leave the room and at that moment there came another sound. This time it was louder, a cross between a growl and a bark.

The aunt turned and looked at Tim.

'There!' she said. 'There it is again.'

'I know,' said Tim. 'My poor stomach is quite empty. If I don't have something to eat it'll make even worse noises.'

The aunt scowled at Tim and made for the door.

'Boys are disgusting,' she said disapprovingly. 'They really are.'

Chapter Four

The next day was a school day. Tim had not planned to take the tin dog to school, but he didn't want to leave him in his room. He knew that his aunt was in the habit of looking in every cupboard for signs of dust and she would be sure to find the tin dog if he were left in the house.

With the tin dog safely tucked away in his school bag, Tim went through the school gates and into his classroom. It was difficult for him to concentrate that morning as all the time he was thinking of his marvellous tin dog and of the things that he would be able to do with him. Halfway through the morning, just to check that the dog was all right, he opened the top of his school bag, which was right underneath his seat. The switch on the dog was still off and the dog seemed to be sleeping peacefully.

Tim was just about to do up the top of the bag again when he heard a whisper from the desk behind him.

'What have you got in there?' his friend, Andrew, asked.

Tim smiled. 'I bet you can't guess,' he said. 'It's something very, very unusual.'

'Please tell me,' said Andrew. 'I won't tell anybody else.'

Tim thought for a moment. He was going to show the tin dog to Andrew anyway, so he might as well tell him now.

'It's a tin dog,' he whispered. 'He behaves just like a real dog, but he's made completely of tin.'

'You're joking,' Andrew sneered. 'There's no such thing as a tin dog.'

'There is,' snorted Tim. 'And I've got one in my bag.'

'Prove it,' whispered Andrew. 'Show me.'

Tim looked towards the end of the classroom. The history teacher was busy writing on the board, so he bent down and opened the bag. Andrew peered over and drew in his breath.

'He's beautiful,' he said. 'Can I hold him?'

Tim looked doubtful.

'Please,' said Andrew. 'I won't break him.'

Carefully, Tim took the tin dog out of the bag and handed him to Andrew. Andrew put him down on the ground beneath his feet and patted the dog's head. As he did so, his hand touched the on/off switch.

With a little jump, the tin dog came to life. Looking round, all he saw was a row of desks and a forest of legs. He could not tell that his master was just in front of him and so, as any dog would do in such a situation, he turned round and bit the leg nearest to him.

Andrew let out a howl as the tin dog gripped his ankle in its tin jaw.

'Ouch!' he shouted. And then again, 'Ouch! Ouch!'

Hearing the noise, the teacher spun round from the board and looked down at the classroom. Some of the others, seeing what was happening, had begun to laugh.

'Now what is happening?' the teacher asked. 'Andrew, was that you shouting out like that?'

'Yow!' answered Andrew. 'I mean, yes. There's a tog, I mean a din tog, I mean a . . .'

'You're talking nonsense,' the teacher said. 'Just sit down and get on with your work.'

The teacher turned round and began writing on the board again. As he did so, Tim swivelled round and seized the tin dog from behind, switching him off as he did so. Then, with the aid of a ruler, he prised open the tin dog's jaws and extracted

Andrew's ankle. Andrew had not been hurt at all, as the tin teeth had not broken the skin. But he was still quite cross and he shook a fist at the tin dog.

'There's no point in doing that,' Tim said. 'He's a tin dog. He doesn't understand.'

Quietly he slipped the tin dog back into his bag and closed the top. He remembered Uncle George's warning. Ankles and rust – those were the things you had to watch out for if you had a tin dog.

'There,' he whispered. 'Now, don't you get into any more trouble.'

On his way home from school, Tim decided that the best thing to do would be to keep the tin dog in the shed at Uncle George's house. He would be safe there, and it would take him no more than five minutes to fetch him whenever he needed him.

Uncle George was pleased to see Tim and his dog when they arrived at the door.

'How is he working?' he asked, bending down to examine the tin dog. 'I see he's got one or two scratches already.'

'That was a cat,' explained Tim. 'And one of the teeth is a little bit bent from where he bit somebody's ankle.'

'That's nothing to worry about,' said Uncle George. 'Tin dogs don't like cats, but cats can't really do anything to harm them. As for ankles – well, I did warn you about that!'

Tim asked his uncle about keeping the dog in the shed.

'That's perfectly all right,' Uncle George replied. 'The shed's a little messy, I'm afraid, but I'm sure the dog won't mind.'

The shed *was* messy. Piled from floor to ceiling were more of Uncle George's bits and pieces – flywheels, springs, cogs, clips, flanges, flinges, divets, widgets – all the equipment he needed to make things. There was just enough room, however, for the tin dog, and together Uncle George and Tim made the dog comfortable on a low shelf.

Uncle George stood back and looked at the dog. As he did so, he scratched his head, making his hair untidier than ever. Tim knew that an idea was coming.

'That dog should be able to run quite fast,' Uncle George said. 'I think we might take him to the dog-racing track one day.'

'To race against real dogs?' Tim asked excitedly.

'I don't see why not,' said Uncle George. 'The rules of dog racing say nothing about tin dogs. And anyway, who would be able to tell?'

Chapter Five

The following day, when Tim went to fetch the tin dog, he found Uncle George in the yard. The tin dog was racing around on the grass, his feet a blur of movement, panting with exertion.

'I'm testing him out,' Uncle George explained. 'And he's every bit as fast as I thought he might be.'

'When will he be ready to race?' Tim asked. 'Will we have to train him?'

Uncle George shook his head. 'He won't need any training,' he said. 'Tin dogs never do.'

He paused, stroking his stubbly chin in a thoughtful way.

'There's a race on this evening,' he mused. 'We could enter him in that.'

The tin dog had now stopped and had trotted over to where Tim was standing. He seemed pleased to see his master and was perched on his hind legs, looking up at Tim.

'Yes,' said Uncle George after a moment's further thought. 'Why not this evening?'

They made their way to the dog-racing track with the tin dog in a special dog-carrying case which Uncle George had unearthed among all the old bits and pieces in the shed. As they approached the track, Uncle George pointed to a special entrance at the side. Painted on a board above it, in large red letters, were the words: OWNERS AND TRAINERS ONLY.

'That's us,' Uncle George said. 'That's where we go in.'

Tim followed Uncle George in through the special entrance. He was extremely excited as he had never been to a dog race before and he had no idea what to expect. It would have been good enough just to watch the race, but to have one's own dog participating made the whole thing even more thrilling. The tin dog was excited, too. He could smell all the other dogs now and he was panting enthusiastically, his tail knocking against the sides of his case.

Uncle George led Tim past several

knots of dog-owners. They were all dressed in much the same way, Tim noticed, with caps pulled down over their eyes, and leads and dog brushes poking out of the pockets of their jackets. One or two of them knew Uncle George and nodded in his direction. This encouraged Tim as he had been wondering whether Uncle George knew anything about dog racing, and now he knew that he must do.

Uncle George joined two men who were standing near the starting gate. He introduced Tim to the men, who nodded in his direction. One of them winked, as if to say, 'I know what you're up to.'

'What sort of dog have you got today, George?' one of the men asked. He was a short man, with bright, sharp eyes

which darted around like a ferret's.

'A good one,' said Uncle George.

'What's he called?' the short man asked.

Uncle George thought for a moment,

'Tinny,' he answered.

'Tiny?' asked the man. 'Is he a small dog then?'

'No,' said Uncle George. 'Tinny.'

'Strange name for a dog, that,' remarked the other man.

'It's a strange dog, this one,' Uncle George said. 'You just wait and see.'

They waited at the side of the track for a few more minutes and then a voice on the loudspeaker announced that the first race was due to begin. At this, Uncle George opened the dog-carrying case and he and Tim let the tin dog jump out. Then, clipping on his lead, they led him to one of the boxes where the dogs waited for the race to begin.

Tim was discouraged by the sight of all the other dogs being entered for the race.

'We haven't got a chance,' he whispered to Uncle George. 'Look at all those greyhounds. They look as if they could outrun a cheetah.'

'Don't give up before you've begun,'
Uncle George said. 'Remember that
this dog is a special one.'

They placed the tin dog in his
starting-box and patted him on the
head.

'Good luck!' Tim said as they walked
back to the barrier. 'Don't let us down.'

The tin dog gave a soft bark and
wagged his tail at Tim. Then he
looked around him, noticing the other
dogs. He seemed not to be at all
nervous, as if this was the sort of thing
that he had done many times before
and which he knew would not be in
the slightest bit difficult.

'They're off!' shouted a voice over the
loudspeaker as the gates sprung up
and the dogs shot out of their boxes.
Tim caught his breath as the gate of
the tin dog's box opened. Where was

the dog? There was no sign of him yet and all the other dogs were well down the track, racing for all their worth after the model rabbit which spun round on its pole to lure them on.

'He's not working,' Tim groaned to his uncle. 'His battery must be flat.'

Uncle George frowned. 'Maybe he doesn't know,' he said. 'Maybe he thinks he's got to stay in the box.'

Just as Uncle George finished speaking, there was a sudden movement in the tin dog's box and then, like an arrow leaving a bow, the tin dog shot out through the gate.

'There he goes!' Uncle George cried out. 'Now just you watch!'

It took the tin dog no more than a few seconds to catch up with the rest of the dogs. Then, pacing himself with the fastest of them, he stayed up at

the front of the runners, his tin legs whizzing backwards and forwards, his head well down.

'Come on!' Tim shouted. 'Overtake them!'

Although all the dogs were now on the far side of the track, it was as though the sound of Tim's voice urged the tin dog to go faster. Putting on a sudden spurt, he leapt forward and was soon several metres in front of the fastest of the real dogs. After a few more moments that distance had increased, and by the time he reached the finishing line the other dogs were well behind him.

'Well done!' Tim cried as he went forward to pick up the tin dog. 'You did it! You won by a mile!'

Chapter Six

There was a short break between the first race and the one that followed it. Together with the other owners, Tim and Uncle George collected their dog from the finishing line and took him back to the side of the track. There were glances from the other owners, some of them admiring, some of them jealous. Everybody had seen how fast the tin dog was and realized that in spite of the fact that he was rather smaller than usual, he would be very hard to beat.

At the side of the track, Uncle George produced a small can of oil and squirted a few drops into the joints of the tin dog's legs. The tin dog seemed to like this as he shook each leg in turn and gave a satisfied grunt.

'That'll feel good,' Uncle George muttered. 'That's what a tin dog likes.'

'He's amazing,' Tim said to his uncle. 'He's at least twice the speed of the other dogs.'

'What did I tell you?' said Uncle George proudly. 'I knew this was a fast one the moment I finished making him.'

Suddenly, Tim became aware that the two men with whom they had talked before the race had now sidled up and were trying to get a closer look at the tin dog. One of them had caught sight of the can of oil and was looking puzzled.

'Fast dog, that,' said the short man, craning his neck to look over Uncle George's shoulder. 'May I take a closer look?'

Tim looked nervously at Uncle George.

'Sorry,' said Uncle George. 'This dog doesn't like people very much. I wouldn't get too close.'

'He doesn't seem to mind you,' retorted one of the men. 'And what did you have in that can?'

Uncle George slipped the oil can back into his pocket.

'My business,' he said, trying to push the tin dog back into his carrying case.

'You running him again?' asked the other, his sharp eyes darting about.

'Yes,' replied Uncle George. 'And if I were you, I'd put my money on him.'

Even as he spoke, Uncle George began to look a little bit worried. The race track was in the open, and although the night had started fine, it was now beginning to rain. It wasn't raining hard enough for the race to be called off, but Tim remembered Uncle George's warning about rust. What would happen to the tin dog if he got wet? He would get rusty. And then what?

The voice on the loudspeaker now announced the second race, and the two men drifted away. Tim and Uncle George lifted up the tin dog, who did not seem in the slightest bit tired, and carried him back to his starting-box.

Once again the tin dog was slow to start, but once again when he shot out of the box it took him no more than a few seconds to catch up with the other dogs and finally to overtake them. This time, when he crossed the finishing line far ahead of all the others, there was a great cheer from the crowd. They had seen his victory in the first race and had all put their money on him in the second. Now they had won, and the tin dog was their hero.

Tim and Uncle George clapped their hands with delight and began to move off towards the finishing line. Then, Tim's heart sank. Something was going very badly wrong. All the other dogs had stopped at the line and were standing panting to get their breath back. The tin dog, though, had not stopped, but was still racing round the track, his legs whirring as fast as ever, his tin ears flattened down for speed.

'What can we do?' Tim asked anxiously. 'Will he ever stop?'

'He'll stop,' Uncle George said, trying to sound confident, but Tim could tell that he too was worried.

The crowd had now noticed that the tin dog was continuing to run and had pressed up to the railings to see the extraordinary sight. No racing dog had ever before carried on after a race and they found the spectacle most amusing.

'That's it, boy,' shouted somebody from the side. 'Just keep going until the next race. Why bother to stop?'

'We'll have to do something,' said Tim. 'He's not going to stop.'

Uncle George nodded his agreement.

'We'll get on to the track,' he said. 'You stand on that side and I'll stand on this. When he comes round again, we'll grab him.'

Tim gulped. The tin dog was still going as fast as ever and Tim wondered whether Uncle George's plan would work. Yet there was nothing else they could do. They could hardly leave the dog racing round the track much longer as the next race was due to start soon and the officials were already beginning to look anxiously at their watches.

Out on the track, Tim crouched down, his arms held wide to stop the tin dog. He could see him approaching now and he tried to position himself so as to be in his way. The tin dog noticed this and swerved to the other side of the track. Tim ran across and spread out his arms again. This time it was too late for the tin dog to cross over again and all he could do was stop or collide with Tim. It may have been that he wanted to stop and couldn't, or it may have been that he didn't want to stop and didn't. Whatever was going on in his tin brain, he ran straight into Tim, who was knocked to the ground by the impact.

An ordinary dog would have been stopped by such a collision, but not the

tin dog. Barely slowing down, he carried on his way, his tin legs moving as fast as before. Down on the ground, Tim felt all the wind knocked out of him. It had been like colliding with an express train, he thought. At least express trains stopped when they knocked you down; the tin dog had no such intention.

The crowd gasped when they saw Tim go down, but when they realized that he was not badly hurt, people began to laugh. Soon they were rocking with laughter, holding their sides, hooting at what was happening. Then, when they saw Uncle George go down too as he tried to stop the tin dog, it was just too much. Strong men wept with laughter, pointing at the dog and its unfortunate owners, enjoying themselves as never before.

Uncle George picked himself up and dusted down his trousers. The crowd had suddenly stopped laughing, and he and Tim wondered what had happened. They turned round to look at the tin dog. They had expected to see him still streaking around the track, but no, that was not what was happening.

The tin dog had slowed down. Now he was only walking, his limbs moving slowly, a grinding noise coming from his insides.

'Rust!' whispered Uncle George. 'The rain has made him rusty.'

Not wasting any time, they both ran in the direction of the tin dog. By the time they reached him, he was barely moving. Little brown rusty streaks of tears were running down his face.

'Is he finished?' asked Tim, as Uncle

George bent down to pick him up.

'I hope not,' said Uncle George. 'But we shall have to see.'

He looked round. People were streaming towards them, all keen to catch a glimpse of the extraordinary dog who was capable of achieving such speed. One of the officials, wearing a white coat and waving a flag, was running towards them shouting something.

'Time to leave,' Uncle George said to Tim, taking him by the arm. 'I think it's probably time to go home.'

Chapter Seven

The tin dog looked rather miserable the next day. Tim helped his uncle lay him out on the workbench and passed him the pliers and the screwdriver when he needed them. He felt sorry for the poor tin dog with his legs so stiff and unmoving, and his mouth that was stuck half-open and half-closed.

Uncle George opened up the tin dog and looked inside.

'Can you fix him?' Tim asked anxiously.

Uncle George poked about the wheels and levers inside.

'There's an awful lot of rust,' he said. 'The rain really soaked him. But I'll try.'

Tim held his breath. He was desperately keen that his dog should be repaired, but he knew that it was touch and go.

Eventually, after more than an hour of probing and prodding, rubbing and polishing, Uncle George screwed the tin dog back together again and turned to Tim.

'He'll work,' he said simply. 'Try him out.'

'I'll take him out for a walk,' Tim suggested. 'That should cheer him up.'

Out on the street, the tin dog

appeared to be working perfectly well. There was nothing wrong with the way his legs moved, and his head was in the right position. But there was something about him that was not yet quite right.

'He's upset about something,' Tim said to Uncle George when he returned to the house. 'There's definitely something wrong.'

Uncle George put the tin dog up on the workbench again and prised open his jaws.

'His tongue looks all right,' he said. 'And the eyes. They seem bright enough.'

He tapped on the tin dog's side.

'That sounds perfect,' he said, shaking his head. 'I really don't know.'

'Perhaps he needs a treat,' Tim said. 'Perhaps that would do the trick.'

Uncle George looked down at Tim and smiled.

'You're right!' he said. 'A treat does a power of good for a tin dog. But . . .' He paused. It was difficult to imagine what the tin dog would really like. Then an idea came to him.

'The circus!' he said. 'That's it! If a circus doesn't cheer you up then nothing will!'

They arrived at the circus in good time and bought their tickets for ringside seats. Inside the tent, the tin dog sat at their feet, his eyes bright with excitement. He lifted his nose to smell all the exciting circus smells. A circus always has a particular sort of smell, the kind which tells you that all sorts of extraordinary things happen there, and for a dog this is the sort of smell which is better than virtually any other.

Before the acts began, the band struck up and the tin dog's ears bristled and twitched. Then, to begin the performance, the ringmaster came in, wearing his splendid red outfit, and this caused the tin dog to let out a little yelp of excitement.

'It's working,' Tim said to Uncle George. 'Look – he's feeling better already.'

'I told you he would,' said Uncle George. 'It always works.'

The first act consisted of some trapeze artists, and the tin dog was not particularly interested in this. When the first animals came in, though, he perked up again and he didn't take his eyes off the elephants and the chimpanzees for one moment. Then there was a clown, who fell about the ring and sprayed everybody with water. The tin dog paid very little attention to this.

'And now!' shouted the ringmaster after the clown had shuffled out of the ring. 'And now we present the star of the show.' He paused for a moment. The lights had been dimmed and the audience was quiet. All that could be heard was the occasional rustle of sweet paper and the crunching of popcorn.

'Ladies and Gentlemen,' the ring-master continued. 'Many circuses have lions, but no circus – other than this one, of course – has a lion which is quite as unusual as ours. No, it is not an Abyssinian lion. No, it is not a giant lion from the Kalahari. No, it is neither of these things.'

'Then what is it?' shouted a voice from the back.

'Yes,' shouted another. 'Tell us. Don't keep us in suspense.'

'I shall tell you,' said the ringmaster, his sparkling white smile flashing in the spotlight. 'Ladies and Gentlemen, prepare yourselves to see . . .' There was a roll of drums and the lights faded further. Then, shooting out into the cage of bars in the middle of the ring, there came a large, frightening creature.

'Ladies and Gentlemen,' shouted the ringmaster. 'The one, the only, the unique – TIN LION!'

Chapter Eight

'I don't believe it,' Tim said to Uncle George.

Uncle George was astonished too.

'I've never seen anything quite like that,' he whispered to Tim. 'I've seen a tin gorilla before, but a tin lion . . .'

They both stared at the magnificent creature. It was certainly larger than an ordinary lion, and its muscles seemed more powerful and rippling. It was a most beautiful colour, a tawny brown, with a mane of gold and deep yellow eyes.

'It's lovely,' Tim exclaimed. 'And listen to its roar.'

The roar was most impressive. Every minute or so, the lion would throw back its head and emit a throaty roar that reverberated up to the top of the great tent and made all the ropes vibrate like the strings of a musical instrument.

'It's a real feat of engineering,' said Uncle George. 'Whoever built that lion must be a genius.'

They watched enraptured as the lion bounded about the cage. Since their seats were at the ringside, they were not far away, and so they had the best possible view of the lion as it ran past them. Everything about it was perfectly finished, down to the ivory claws which were neatly stuck in the bottom of the feet.

Tim and his uncle were so enthralled by the tin lion that they totally forgot about the tin dog. And because of this, they did not notice the tin dog slipping off and making his way to the very edge of the ring. By the time they noticed him it was too late. With one jump, the tin dog was in the ring, heading straight for the lion's cage.

If the tin dog had been a little bit fatter he would not have been able to get through the bars. But as it was, perhaps because of all the exercise he had been getting, he was thin enough to slip through the bars. With a growing sense of horror, Tim and his uncle saw their tin dog leap into the

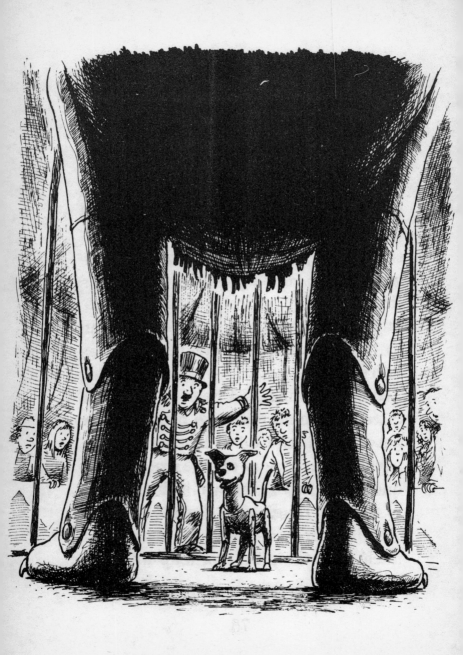

lion's cage and go straight over towards where the lion was standing.

When the lion noticed the tin dog, it stood quite still. Unconcerned, the tin dog gave a friendly bark and trotted over the sawdust floor, his tail wagging in friendliness.

'Get that dog out of there!' the ringmaster cried. 'Quick, before it's too late!'

Uncle George rose to his feet and called out to the tin dog. But it was already too late. Before the tin dog could realize what was happening, the giant tin lion had opened its great jaws, pounced, and swallowed him up completely. Then the lion sat back, licked its lips and roared loudly.

'Uncle!' screamed Tim. 'My dog! My dog!'

'Keep calm,' soothed Uncle George. 'I'll see if I can save him.'

'But he's gone!' wailed Tim. 'He's been eaten by a great lion. It's all over.'

'No,' said Uncle George. 'I'm afraid that the excitement is only just beginning!'

At the back of the tent, Uncle George went straight up to the lion-keeper, who had just prodded the tin lion back into its caravan cage.

'Your lion ate our tin dog,' he complained. 'Everybody saw it.'

'I know,' said the keeper. 'I'm terribly sorry, but your dog shouldn't have rushed into the ring like that.'

'I know,' said Uncle George. 'But he's only a tin dog, and he doesn't really know any better.'

'And my lion is only a tin lion,' said

the keeper. 'It doesn't know any better either.'

Uncle George looked up into the lion's cage. The tin lion was prowling around, still roaring, looking quite contented now that its belly was full of the tin dog.

'Can't you switch it off?' he asked the keeper. 'Then we could do something about getting the dog out.'

The keeper shook his head sadly.

'Its switch has been broken for weeks,' he said. 'And it's powered by very long-lasting batteries. It probably won't run down for at least four months.'

'Four months!' exclaimed Uncle George. 'Then how do we get our dog back?'

'There's only one way,' said the keeper. 'Somebody goes in there and tries to reach its emergency switch.'

'Well,' said Uncle George in a firm tone. 'That's exactly what you should do.'

The keeper looked pale. 'Oh no,' he said. 'Not me. I was thinking of *you*.'

Chapter Nine

'Oh no!' said Uncle George hotly. 'You're not getting me in there!'

Tim looked at his uncle. Then he looked at the lion, at its great claws and its powerful jaws, and he knew exactly what Uncle George meant. And yet, inside that lion was his tin dog . . .

'Well,' he said, trying to sound brave. 'It'll have to be me. I'll go in.'

'Nonsense,' snapped the keeper.

'You wouldn't last two minutes.'

'Quite right,' agreed Uncle George. 'You stay where you are.'

'But somebody has to rescue the tin dog,' Tim protested. 'And nobody else is willing.'

Uncle George looked at Tim and swallowed hard.

'I made that dog,' he said. 'I suppose I'd better go in.'

'Well done,' exclaimed the keeper, looking most relieved. 'Now, if you listen to me for a moment, I'll tell you exactly what you should do . . .'

The tin lion watched suspiciously as the keeper opened the door of its cage. He opened it just wide enough for Uncle George to slip through and then he slammed it shut again and fastened the catch. The lion did nothing at first, but when it saw that

Uncle George was inside the cage it gave a low, warning growl.

Uncle George stood still. The lion stood still. Outside, Tim felt as if his limbs were frozen. Then, very slowly, Uncle George began to cross the cage towards the tin lion. For a moment the lion watched him, its large yellow eyes narrowed, the whiskers round its vast mouth twitching ever so slightly.

'Now,' whispered the keeper.

Uncle George began to creep forward, watched by the lion. Suddenly there was a great roar, and the bars of the cage shook and rattled. Uncle George ducked his head and leapt towards the tin lion, which had by now begun to circle him. There was a flurry of limbs, mane, feet, and untidy hair. There was another roar and the sound of a fist beating against tin.

'Go for the switch!' shouted the keeper. 'Watch out for its teeth!'

Tim held his breath. He knew that Uncle George was trying to reach the emergency switch which the keeper had told him was to be found underneath the lion's chest, but would he do so before the great jaws managed to tear him to pieces?

'Oh dear!' shouted the keeper. 'I

don't think he's going to be able to do it!'

Horrified, Tim saw that the tin lion had got the better of his uncle. Uncle George had failed to reach the switch in time, and the lion was standing above him, licking its lips. Then the jaws opened, and Uncle George was looking up into a mouthful of gleaming, white lion teeth.

Tim closed his eyes. There was nothing he could do. This was the end of his uncle. When he opened his eyes again, he saw that part of Uncle George had disappeared. Half of him was still there — the lower half, sticking out of the tin lion's mouth — but the rest had been swallowed.

'Oh, my goodness!' wailed the keeper. 'This is the worst day of my life!'

'And of mine!' came a muffled voice from inside the cage.

'Uncle George!' Tim cried. 'Are you all right?'

'Yes,' came the faint reply from within the lion.

'What can we do?' Tim shouted. 'How can we help?'

'You can fetch me a screwdriver,' Uncle George replied.

The keeper rushed off and within seconds was back with a screwdriver. Tim snatched it from him, opened the door of the cage and approached the lion. Of course, the lion could do very little, as it had Uncle George's feet sticking out of its mouth and that made it rather difficult for it to move its head.

'Are you there?' Uncle George called out, his voice sounding a little fainter.

'Don't waste any time.'

Tim stood beside the lion. It growled at him, and it also tried to swipe at him with one of its paws, but it was too distracted by the legs in its mouth to do much else. Tim dodged the paw and waited for his uncle to tell him what to do.

Suddenly a bulge appeared in the side of the lion. Then there was a banging sound and a moment after that a tin panel popped open and a hand shot out. Tim put the screwdriver into his uncle's hand and then ran to the other side of the cage. The lion was becoming angry, and was eyeing Tim hungrily. Ignoring the legs and the heavy weight in its stomach, it was now beginning to pace towards Tim.

'Get out!' shouted the keeper. 'If

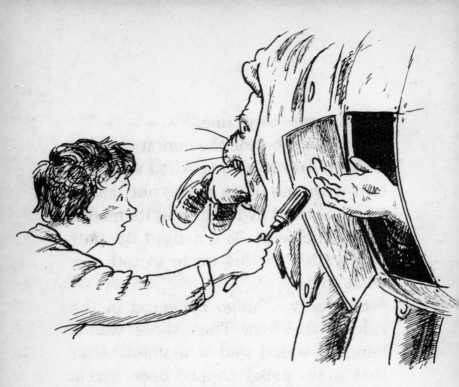

those claws get you, they'll rip you to bits in no time.'

Tim looked frantically about him. He realized that he should have gone towards the front of the cage and not towards the back. Now he was trapped.

From within the lion there came the sound of activity. There was a metallic banging and, Tim thought, a bark. He looked at the lion. It was now only a couple of metres away from him and there was no escape. Tim looked down at the floor so that he would not have to see those dreadful claws as they flashed towards him.

'Good!' shouted a voice. 'That should do it.'

Tim looked up. The great tin lion was frozen still, one of its paws, claws extended, stopped in mid-air. Uncle George had succeeded in turning it off from inside. They were safe.

By the time Uncle George had removed a further tin panel from the side of the lion, the ringmaster had arrived and was surveying the scene. The keeper explained to him what had happened, and the ringmaster shook his head anxiously.

'That lion,' he said crossly, 'has been more trouble than it's worth.'

With the panel removed, Uncle George was able to wiggle out of the side of the lion. Tim helped him and, his feet disappearing through the lion's mouth, he was soon entirely out. Tim hugged his uncle with relief.

'I thought you were gone,' he said. 'I thought it was all over.'

'Almost,' said Uncle George. 'But not quite.'

He turned to the lion again and put his hand through the hole where the panel had been. Then he peered in, called out, and stood to one side.

With a cheerful bark, his tail wagging energetically, out popped the tin dog. When he saw Tim, he bounded up to him and bounced into his arms.

'You're safe!' cried Tim. 'You're safe at last!'

The ringleader watched all this with interest.

'What a remarkable dog,' he said. 'How very strange this all is.'

The ringmaster invited them into his caravan for a hot drink and a plate of sandwiches.

'I really am most relieved this has had a happy ending,' he said. 'It would have been terrible if you hadn't got out.'

'I agree,' said Uncle George. 'But I did get out, and so did our tin dog. And that's all that matters.'

The ringmaster looked thoughtful.

'That dog,' he said, pointing to the tin dog. 'He can obviously do all sorts of tricks.'

'Oh yes,' said Tim. 'He's remarkably clever.'

'Mmm,' mused the ringmaster. 'A dog like that would do very well in a circus.'

For a moment nothing was said. Tim glanced at his uncle, and Uncle George glanced at the tin dog, who was glancing at the plate of sand-wiches.

'I'll make you an offer for that dog,' said the ringmaster. 'It'll be a generous offer.'

Uncle George shook his head.

'That dog's not for sale,' he said. 'He belongs to Tim.'

The ringmaster smiled. 'In that case,' he said. 'How about joining the circus? All three of you?'

Uncle George put his cup down on the table. 'Are you serious?' he asked.

'Yes,' said the ringmaster. 'You look as if you'd be a pretty good handyman to have about the place. We don't have anybody to fix things at the moment. And you,' he said, turning to face Tim, 'you could train that dog for his act. We could get some other performing dogs – real ones – to go into the ring with him. I've had enough of that tin lion. Its parts are all worn out now. It's time it was sent to the scrap heap.'

Tim waited for Uncle George to reply. He didn't have to wait long.

'I think that's a very good idea,'

Uncle George said. 'How about you, Tim? It would mean that you could come and live with me.'

'I'd love that,' Tim said. 'But what about . . . what about Aunt Mag?'

Uncle George looked thoughtful.

'She thinks my home is terribly messy,' he said, 'and that would probably make her want to say no. But . . .'

Tim looked at his uncle expectantly. Did he have an idea for persuading Aunt Mag?

Uncle George was smiling.

'Yes!' he said. 'That's it! I've been meaning to finish that domestic robot for years. Now I shall do it!'

'Domestic robot?' asked Tim. 'What's that?'

'It's a tin cleaning lady,' answered Uncle George. 'She has a tin bucket and a tin mop. When you turn on the switch, she whizzes round the house and cleans it up. The whole place will be spick and span in no time at all – and it will stay that way!'

Tim laughed. If Uncle George lived in a clean home, then Aunt Mag could have no objection to letting him live there too. And he would have such fun, especially with his friend the tin dog. He looked at the tin dog and thought of some of the tricks he could teach him. He could hardly wait to start.

THE END

SUZY MAGICIAN

by Alexander McCall Smith

'ABRACADABRA!'

There is nothing in the world that Suzy wants more than to be a magician – the best ever.

When a chance comes up to win a place at Professor Cadabra's world-famous magic school, Suzy practises her most difficult tricks for the competition. But she needs a trick or two up her sleeve when things don't turn out quite as expected . . .

SBN 0 552 526061

If you would like to receive a Newsletter about our new Children's books, just fill in the coupon below with your name and address (or copy it onto a separate piece of paper if you don't want to spoil your book) and send it to:

The Children's Books Editor
Transworld Publishers Ltd.
61-63 Uxbridge Road,
Ealing
London W5 5SA

Please send me a Children's Newsletter:

Name...

Address...

....

....

All Children's Books are available at your bookshop or newsagent, or can be ordered from the following address:
Corgi/Bantam Books,
Cash Sales Department,
P.O. Box 11, Falmouth, Cornwall TR10 9 EN

Please send a cheque or postal order (no currency) and allow 80p for postage and packing for the first book plus 20p for each additional book ordered up to a maximum charge of £2.00 in UK.

B.F.P.O. customers please allow 80p for the first book and 20p for each additional book.

Overseas customers, including Eire, please allow £1.50 for postage and packing for the first book, £1.00 for the second book, and 30p for each subsequent title ordered.